Lúnasa Days

a novella of corn, fate, and the end of summer

DREW JACOB

Library of Congress Cataloging-In-Publication Data
Lúnasa days / Drew Jacob — 1st ed.
ISBN: 978-0-9920059-4-8
eISBN: 978-0-9920059-5-5
WC: 14,937
1. Fate. 2. Summer. 3. Lúnasa. 4. Magic. 5. Corn.

Cover design by Zack Whitley
Editing provided generously by Miya Kressin
Additional editing by Doan Phuong Nguyen

Author info:
Website: roguepriest.net
Twitter: @Rogue_Priest

My Patrons

This Book would not have been written without the financial and moral support of a small number of dedicated patrons.

You took a gamble on a young writer with nothing but a story and a bike. You are more than patrons of the arts—you are my personal saviors.

Angel Avery
Ty Barabary
Sarah Cool
Dawn Marie Costorf
Niall Doherty
Sharla Donohue
Caroline Fautsch
Trent Fowler
Urban Haas & Suamya Arya Haas
Bruce Harroun & Ellen Hachey

Sean Holt
Kate Jacob
Melissa Ann Judy
Scot McIntosh
Stuart North
Morpheus Ravenna
Wayne Ross
Linda Slack
Beth Varro
Zack Whitley

Thank you.

Lúnasa Days

This is a story of Fate,

The wind of alchemy.

You will feel it when it gusts. It may come like a storm; it may come like a whisper. You can ride it, you know, like seeds on the wind, cotton willow on the wind.

You can ride it, but you may not land.

Part One:
Bailey

1

The sun's going. It's July, and the corn doesn't know it. It grows tall and green. The human heart knows. It stirs and it stirs.

There's a dwindling late in summer, a sadness. And a loner on the roads.

He left a life that wasn't bad. Everyone said he was good at his job, even his boss.

But when he was young he knew something. He had a fate, a reason to exist. He never quite found it, and every autumn it slipped further away.

He stopped one day for food. A gas station, like any other, but the man there was friendly. Bored. He liked the look of the young guy with his bike, and he spoke to him.

"Where you headed?"

It was a hard question.

"Well, what do you do?"

Vagabond. Can you say vagabond? Is that a career?

He looked aside.

"I cast spells," he said.

The man had some work for him.

2

Once, Bailey worked in marketing. It was not what he wanted.

He went to school for it. Why? To make money. That is the great purpose in life.

And Bailey did make a little money. Not as much as he was told. He took the internship, the entry level, the promotion, and the new employer. He had enough to spend. Cocktails, theater, road trip. Reward.

Most weekends were road trips. He left work early—the boss didn't mind. He drove hours on a highway. Sometimes he camped, sometimes he got a room. It was exciting, once. It felt like exploration. There was always a new town to see.

Until you run out.

How many highways are there? How far can you run on a long-weekend leash? A day out, a day there, a day back.

There are byways of course. They too have limits.

Bailey had seen every little town and state park he could reach. He revisited. He knew where to get coffee, bakery, tap beer. He took new girlfriends to the same bistros he took old girlfriends. Mostly he went alone.

And there was a bigger problem, one named Sunday.

Even with reruns, Friday meant excitement. He bounced to

the car, sang loud as he drove, and made friends easily. In a word: release.

Whatever he let out had to be canned again. Sunday he willingly, obediently returned. If only he was blameless! But it was his consent, his own feet that brought him back.

He conspired in his own unhappiness.

3

He felt Fate very close, once. A granddad with one hand on his shoulder. He whispered quietly, pointed, smiled. "Do you see that? Over there, boy, over there!"

He was 17 years old.

How does one begin casting spells? It's different for every magician. Some find it in a book. Some learn from a teacher. Some seek it out, others have it shoved upon them.

Bailey tripped into it.

He'd wanted a book on the Greek gods. He didn't know the one he grabbed was meant for practitioners. The woman at the counter appraised him. She sold him the book but said, in a kindly way: don't use the dark stuff.

He read it all that night.

Reading does not make you a magician. It requires practice. Half of Bailey strained to try it; half of him sneered. It *can't* work.

Can it?

He set about building a shrine. He hid this from his parents. Trinkets from junk shops. It looked baroque, ceremonial.

One night he cut a wand of willow under moonlight. He followed all the prescriptions, approached his shrine, chanted.

He felt foolish.

But he continued. He said the words and made the motions. At every step he expected that nothing would happen. Nothing, and he was stupid for trying.

Then something happened.

The world opened. Something was *with* him. His eyes went wide. He told himself it was his imagination. Then he bowed.

If there are gods, this was a god. He had called to Apollo, and Apollo answered.

There was no shower of sparks, no glowing fog or shaking earth. Bailey didn't *see* anything. But it grabbed him. On his knees Bailey could hear his own pulse, galloping.

Why did Bailey chant that night? So he could make offerings and ask for something. Instead he held communion.

The thoughts in his head came from somewhere else. He received answers faster than he could form questions. The voice was neither kind nor cruel. It was direct.

His moment with Apollo was short. He came away knowing: if you're going to do this, do it right. Otherwise quit.

Bailey did not quit.

In that moment, Bailey discovered both magic and religion. He still had his doubts—imagination?—but he couldn't forget what he felt. As his deity ordered, he studied before he tried again. It was a long time before he did. But at his next ritual, he was prepared.

4

Magic is yelling in the dark.

Anyone lost might try it. They don't really expect an answer. Who could be out there? When a voice yells back, they run.

When Bailey heard the voice, he stopped yelling and listened. He contemplated his options. And he walked toward it.

His second ceremony was very different. He had studied magic. He thought about his deity as *real*, and he wanted to be respectful.

Magic, he now knew, was not a bribe to the gods. It had technique, method, science. He could learn these things and not pester Apollo for every little charm.

But he hadn't learned *yet*. So that day he went pestering.

The offerings were more substantial. The ceremony more elegant. He knew what to say; he had planned the words carefully.

He began.

The candles, the invocation, the chanting were all fine. He was more confident. But at the peak of his chant he did not feel the world open. No great presence swept before him, nothing threw him off his feet.

Hesitation.

Novice hands put the offerings on the shrine. He knelt, closed his eyes. There was something there. It felt faraway.

"Apollo?"

Hmm.

The god was watching, he thought.

Bailey began his practiced request. He needed training, help. He needed a mentor.

He asked Apollo to teach him.

Laughter.

Good natured laughter, an athlete at his teammates. But laughter. The words came clear in Bailey's head:

"I already am."

At that moment he heard his bedroom door. Bailey was sure of it. He heard the noise and turned, on his feet. But the door was still closed.

Something brushed his leg. He looked. There was nothing.

Empty as the room was, Bailey knew that a little dog had entered. A little white dog, or something that looked like one. It was the first time Bailey saw something with total certainty in his mind's eye. This was, itself, a lesson.

That spirit, the first he ever sensed, would become his familiar. And Apollo, for his part, was a distant teacher.

5

He learned two things about his familiar: it was more like a wolf than a dog, and it had a name.

The name Bailey called it was Aximander. Whether he had chosen the name for it, or whether the spirit told him that was its name, was never clear.

The uncertainty bothered him. On the night of the ceremony Bailey completely believed that his experience was real, that there truly was a spirit there beside him, and that something momentous had happened. But by morning he wasn't sure.

The struggle of *knowing* became a battle.

He read books. Dozens of them. They gave no answers. The ones that taught magic simply assumed it was real. They took it on faith.

Bailey had no faith. He had curiosity. He didn't just want to feel magic; he wanted to prove it.

And Aximander? The spirit approved. It gave them a reason to enchant. Bailey held ceremonies whenever he could hide them from his parents. The rest of the time he read. He always had some new technique to try. One week he'd be floating out of his body, another week painting sigils.

The two grew close.

Bailey didn't have many friends. He didn't know how to talk to his own age. Real or not, Aximander became a comfort. Bailey thought of the spirit as male, and felt the spirit get bigger, grow stronger as they worked together.

They began to get results.

6

Magic does not grant wishes. It does not slay demons or change the color of the sky. Magic is very subtle.

In college, this suited Bailey.

The professor who changed a grade on second thought. The extra commission at his part-time job. The girl who never noticed him, then suddenly did.

These are small effects. They take time to bring about. Sometimes a ceremony seemed like too much work for too little result. Bailey worked on that. He enjoyed calling to spirits. Where others would have given up, he dove deeper.

He had the time.

His job wasn't demanding; he skipped a lot of homework; business school isn't hard, if you know how to bluff. So he walked in forested gullies and sang, or hunted for bird skulls to use in his charms.

His friends were divided. Some loved it. They always wanted a spell, some advice from the guy with the spirits. He wasn't dreamy or gullible, he was easy to talk to and he knew his art.

Other friends thought it was all in his head. He had coffee with them and loud, fierce debates. Neither side had fun, but both sides wanted a rematch. Young men must have their bull fight.

Old men do not. At first Bailey disregarded the criticism of his professors. He made the same arguments to them that he made at the coffee house. They weren't moved. Magic was beneath even arguing with.

In four years he learned: to succeed, hide your beliefs.

Most people learn this lesson either too young or too late. Bailey learned it just as he entered his career.

7

The greatest mistake you can make is to believe Fate will arrive all on its own. Bailey made this mistake.

He had no particular idea of what to do after graduation. He knew what he wanted: respect, solitude, a lover with very dark eyes. And he was willing to work some high-paying job to get there.

The university career advisor had a less gilded vision for Bailey. He explained the sort of jobs people start in, and how to get them. He saw that Bailey had done little networking and little preparation. He suggested *realistic* openings.

Was the advisor a realist? No. Not more than Bailey was. Bailey saw the world too bright, but across the desk the man saw it too dim. His mission was to pop grandiose beliefs, to deflate graduates to a more manageable size. He was rewarded for a high placement rate—in other words, if students settled.

Bailey refused the openings he suggested. The man could only tell him to hunt on his own. So Bailey went before Apollo.

It was evening. He spent the day getting ready. He made offerings and went into communion.

In real magic, no words are heard. Nothing materializes. But Bailey spoke.

"I'm living off a loan. Apollo, I'm afraid."
Silence.
"What do I do?"
But there was only silence.

8

Few things have a predictable effect on a human soul. A career is one of them. Bailey's career did what every career does: it cropped off the extremes. A job never creates happiness, but some create contentment. So the corners of Bailey's life disappeared. His basic needs were guaranteed and his highest aspirations pruned.

The working professional always has a friend. You are handlers of the same beast. You can complain together, commiserate about the irony of life.

This then *becomes* life.

Bailey joined in. He spent most nights—most money— eating and drinking with his friends. None of them had much, neither wealth nor respect. The nights *had* to be fun, because if they weren't, what was the point of the job?

He took very little time for magic. With his busy new life he set a once-a-week time to make sure he practiced. Even this was compromised.

Aximander didn't forget him. Neglected, the spirit began to shrink. He appeared less and less. But he remained, still awaiting ceremony. When Bailey took the time for offerings he sensed a sadness from his companion. He felt guilty.

So he offered even less.

Did he speak of it to his coworkers? Never. He learned from his professors. Sometimes over beer the topic of ghosts or spirits would come up. He suddenly had an opinion that sounded studied and convinced. His friends pushed for details. He drew back and became coy.

They wrote this off as eccentricity. It was the least eccentric he'd ever been.

For twentyish he was reliable. He didn't make the usual mistakes of bad taste and poor judgment. Instead he committed the greater mistake of self-betrayal—and he worked hard. His employer didn't notice; he found a new employer. With it, new friends. In four weeks all the old ones had forgotten him.

Bailey became successful. His income rose, his bills rose. More people respected him, more controlled him. He had that special curse: responsibility.

Magic went from an art to a hobby. Finally, to a memory. He still made offerings to Apollo. They were routine.

He was the young man with a promising future. It was what he asked for, and what he chased. Men five years older were jealous. Younger ones scoffed: he had sold out. Perhaps they too were jealous.

This is normal for a success story. What is not normal is to give it up.

9

"Where you headed?"

The man nodded toward Bailey's bike. It leaned against the gas station window. He was the only customer there.

He didn't know where he was going.

Not answering felt awkward. The old man didn't notice. He just wanted conversation, so he kept going.

"Well, what do you do?"

Bailey almost cracked a joke. "Vagabond." It's what he'd told everyone so far. But those were people he knew: people who wanted to know what his next step was. It was a good answer, a dodge.

Now he was past the towns he knew. His road trips had never taken him this far. The bartenders, the café owners no longer remembered his face.

And he *wasn't* a vagabond. A vagabond has no purpose and no destination. Bailey had no destination, but he was sure he had a purpose. At least to himself.

He hadn't tried telling anyone else.

You don't know this guy. You'll never see him again.

That thought gave him courage.

"I cast spells."

The man's head turned. He had only been making chit chat. He squinted, made sure he'd heard right. Then he leaned back.

"What kind of spells?"

It was Bailey's turn to look up. No laughter, no dismissal. Just an honest question. Bailey still felt embarrassed to answer, and that made him seem sincere.

"I— well. Whatever kind you need. I've been doing this for over ten years."

That was credentials enough for the gas station man. Do you ask a wizard for his resumé? He handed Bailey his change.

"Thing is, it's been hard times. Can you do anything about that?"

Reaching for the change, their hands met. So did their eyes. The man's held worry. Deep worry, and loss.

It snapped Bailey immediately out of his embarrassment. This wasn't about him. There were *problems*.

"Tell me about it," he said.

The gas man laid out his troubles. He owned his gas station independently. A larger place had opened on the main highway. With their diner and ice cream cones his business had dropped.

At one point, another customer came in. The man broke off. He knew the other customer, and they talked for twenty minutes. It drove Bailey crazy. He was used to the pace of a city: let's finish this meeting, and get started. But he waited.

At last they were alone. Bailey had been thinking about the problem.

"I'll do three spells for you," he said. "One on the cash register, one behind the counter, and one out front."

The man was still worried. "People gonna see it?"

Bailey shook his head.

The man nodded. "What do I have to pay you?"

Bailey paused. He was unsure. He wanted to say "whatever you want," but he knew from experience how that would go. He said a number.

"Fifty dollars."

The man thought a long time.

"Deal."

Bailey went to his bicycle. He had expected balking, bargaining. Not trust.

It's the spells he trusts, came the thought from his familiar.

Bailey cringed.

10

How do you enchant a gas station?

Bailey wasn't sure.

He had no plan in particular. He had made up on the spot everything he'd said about three spells. A magician does not have a book with answers. Some have recipes; Bailey didn't even have that. He had a small collection of odd things.

On the back of his bicycle were saddlebags. One contained a box. It was a different color than the first aid kit. He opened this box and surveyed its contents.

Some paints and brushes. Red pepper and salt. A bag of sand. Four vials of colored liquid. A stack of blank note cards. Whiskey.

Well, the whiskey was low. It had not been used for spells.

As he got these things Bailey spoke silently to Aximander. The spirit declined to answer.

"Oh, come *on*," he urged.

"You're lucky I'm even here."

"I'll do it myself."

He closed his kit. The gas station man stood in the doorway, watching. He had paid for a show. But Bailey wasn't ready.

"I'll need some time to prepare."

The man nodded.

Bailey tried to go past him. He didn't seem to notice.

"Excuse me." He nudged his way back inside.

Soon he was locked in the bathroom.

He was there for thirty minutes. For ten of them he panicked. How to do these spells? Why did the man trust him? What if he couldn't deliver?

He thought about the likely outcome of the spells. The gas station really was at a poor location. The only reason Bailey had found it was because he liked quiet country highways. But bicyclists don't buy gas.

So the gas station would, eventually, close. Bailey doubted his spell would change that.

But life support? How much of an uptick in sales could a spell manage—how many extra people might turn left instead of right, take the scenic route, add a newspaper and a coffee at the last minute?

What if I'm ripping him off?

The next ten minutes were spent just calming himself down.

"Filthy." It was Aximander, in his head.

Bailey looked around. It was. There was no daily cleaning. The floor drain stank. The walls were stained. He sat on the toilet seat because there was nowhere else to sit. He felt a need to wipe it off first.

He meditated there.

The final ten minutes he got ready. He washed his hands and his face. He drew marks in the grime on the mirror. He planned his ceremony. Aximander was silent.

When he came out a customer was just leaving. The gas man looked at Bailey, and Bailey grabbed a small bottle of whiskey from the shelf. "I'm using a little of this."

He didn't wait for an answer. He took a soda cup, and the whiskey, and he went outside.

He lifted a gas nozzle and sprayed a blast into the soda cup. It soaked his hand and shirt. Aximander laughed.

"Fuck you!" He said it out loud. But he laughed too. There had to be sacrifice. He opened the whiskey, and offered some. His familiar took the aspect of a large white wolf cub, and lapped it up.

Bailey drank some himself. He knew the gas man was watching, and he didn't care. But he spat whiskey into the cup of gasoline. *There's your show.*

He walked to the road and waited till there were no cars. It didn't take long. Carefully, slowly, he poured the gas-whiskey in a large sigil on the pavement. It was sloppy work, to be sure, but that didn't matter. He oriented it so that the top pointed at the gas station. Instinctively, he knew what he needed to do.

He needed to light it on fire.

He debated. The gas pumps were over a hundred feet away. There was no wind. But it didn't feel safe.

"Do it."

Bailey shook his head. What would he tell the police, if he blew it up? The owner paid me to do it?

"Do it!"

"No."

He walked back into the gas station.

"Here's the rest of your whiskey."

"How does this all work?"

"By chance. Coincidence. The odds bend in your favor." Suddenly he had a doctor's manner, total confidence. "You won't wake up rich tomorrow, but business will improve."

"That's good enough for me."

Bailey nodded. He came behind the counter. There were no customers, so he started right there. He painted a small sigil on a note card, and as he did he sang some words over it. He took back the bottle of whiskey, even though he had given it up, and splashed some around the card.

And dusted sand on it.

The sand smudged some paint. He made the gas man open the register, and blew in colored sand. Then he walked backwards from register to door, blowing a breath of sand with every step.

He thought he'd be embarrassed. The truth is, it felt good.

The last sand was scattered out the door. He picked up his paints again, and repainted the first sigil. This time he mixed some colored liquid in it, and the words he said were longer.

"Bring the money."

The man got it out of the register.

"Now we shake hands over this symbol, and then you hand me the money over it."

They did that.

Bailey pressed the money onto the wet paint, turned it over, and blew across it at the man.

"Let this symbol dry and then keep it behind the counter. You can hide it if you want."

The man nodded. He seemed struck. But he spoke.

"Wait."

His grabbed the half-bottle of whiskey. Bailey noticed, for the first time, how pocked his old hands were.

"You can have this, too."

By accident or intent, he handed it to Bailey across the symbol. That felt right.

"Thanks. Is there anywhere good to camp around here?"

Part of him hoped the old man's kindness would extend

even further: a place to sleep. But their business was concluded.

The old man gave him directions to a campground "up the road." He said it was ten miles, but he drove a truck. Bailey knew he was lucky if it was fifteen.

He thanked the man, and went out the door.

The bicycle took eight minutes to get ready. The sky said evening was coming. He'd been there a long time, doing spells, and he was behind schedule. Aximander pawed around the tall grass.

At the gas station entrance, Bailey paused. He could see the dampness where his gas-and-whiskey diagram was. He took his lighter and flicked it, holding a flame to the pavement. Of course, by now, it wouldn't light. He touched fire to the four corners of the sigil, and asked Apollo to bless the old man.

The blessing had to come from somewhere.

11

Had the road freed Bailey, as he hoped? In a way. The stresses he once felt were gone. A dull, daily anxiety was deleted. In its place were extremes: the pleasure of total freedom, the terror of what tomorrow holds.

It was later than Bailey thought. He went through a tiny town, no bigger than a few buildings at a bygone crossroad. He asked someone if there was a motel nearby. There was not. What about the campground? They disagreed on where to go.

He spotted a country church. No one was there, not in the evening. He kept going.

Evening came and he resolved to knock on a door. He had never actually done this before. So far on his trip he had planned every day to end somewhere he could stay: either camp or rent a room. He was nervous about approaching a stranger. But he told himself he would do it.

The mind is tricky.

That house looks too rough, too worn down. *That* one has kids; they have their hands full enough already. He kept telling himself he'd go to the next one.

Then were wasn't a next one.

How long do you hold out? When do you turn back? If it's

been twenty minutes with no houses, is the next one just a few minutes further? What if it's been *forty* minutes?

He saw industrial buildings, sometimes. Strange structures that could be for processing grain or refining chemicals for all he knew. He did see one farmhouse, but clearly no one was home. Mostly he saw just fields.

A truck went past. He felt a cold and irrational anger because they didn't stop and offer to help.

The sun was hardly still up. To turn back to past homes now would take nearly an hour, and who brings in strangers after dark? Bailey's priorities changed. He would take a shed, an empty barn, a haystack, a windbreak.

Up ahead was a line of trees. And perhaps a little vacation cabin?

No. Only trees.

He dismounted. Walked the bike to the edge. Looked both ways on the road. There was no one to help him, and no one to stop him.

So he entered the little wood. Yes, this would do. He could camp here.

There was a tent bag on the back of his bike. It was an old dome tent from the last century. He hadn't wanted to spend money on a bivouac. But the tent took time to set up. It needed a clear space to sit in. It was awkward and a lot of work.

Bailey was tired. He didn't want to set up a tent in the dark.

Even moving the bike was hard. The woods were thick with undergrowth. The spokes tangled and the tires stuck in ruts. He got it hidden, though, and wrestled his sleeping bag from it.

The mosquitoes began.

He went to the edge of the wood, where it would be windier. Mosquitoes don't like wind. But then, many of them are brave.

There he sat, under a tree. He wrapped the bedroll around himself and gazed at corn stalks, swaying in the breeze, rustling.

Twice a minute tiny wings whined in his ear. He made an offering, trying to be thankful for his new free life, and ate some food. It didn't taste good. But he gulped water.

Out in the field it was quiet. Occasionally some sudden commotion, then the silence again. Plus the crickets, the buzzing, the hum. That didn't bother him. Twice, three times a minute—that bothered him.

The tree had had chosen was a good shape, though. He leaned his head softly against it. How bad would his neck be in ten hours?

It began to rain.

12

There's a special kind of unconsciousness reserved for soldiers, prisoners and stupid young men who walk in the wild.

To say Bailey *fell asleep* is inaccurate. He fell nowhere. Sleep was like a fresh-dug grave beneath him, one he kept leaping out of before he was buried in. He lost sense of the passage of time, like he was floating. But he tumbled awake and he tumbled awake.

The tree made his back sore. The rain stopped, but the cold remained.

Sleep is a mistress. She doesn't ask much, but she's impatient. She *begged* for Bailey. He was unable to accept—and like any woman worth kissing, eventually she moved on.

He was sure many hours had passed. He looked at his phone.

Seven hours till dawn.

Part Two:
Emily

13

Emily had problems of her own.

It was a fine morning. Sunny. Dry.

She knew she had to go but she stared out the window. There were clouds—actual clouds. Clouds can bring rain. She had no hope for these clouds. They didn't *smell* like rain.

They all heard the pitter-patter last night. Unlike anyone, she didn't get up. She didn't run outside. She didn't sit nervous to know how much fell. She just listened to the sound, the comforting sound, and went back to sleep.

But the earth did not look dark and damp like coffee grounds. The grass was not matted nor dewed. It could have been a photograph of yesterday, or any day before.

And she really didn't care anymore.

She did know, however, that something was going to break. And it would break hard.

She looked back at the cards in front of her. Every Sunday she drew her card. She read for the week ahead. Once it was daily, with a full spread. Then she fell in love, and it changed everything.

Love is not good for little girls. It is poison and intoxicant. When Kore ate the seed she died for half a year. Real girls don't die for half a year. Real girls die.

But this card had cock and balls on full display. And a grin. Red skin, princely horns, a lazy erection.

She looked out the window again. The face on the card kept smiling.

The Devil.

14

Emily had always seen things. In the beginning it was pretend, it was normal. Mom and Dad were proud of their creative little girl.

But creative little girls scare serious adults.

The things she spoke of were Not Okay. It was one thing when it was Grandma, a year after she died. It was another when it was Jesus, saying he didn't like church.

Or the neighbor's dead dad.

And it was all mixed together. Not just these ominous, confident declarations. Imaginary lands and make-believe critters. The talking frog! She always did love her talking frog.

Emily had not seen a frog talk in over five years.

The tarot cards didn't bother them. Actually it was a relief— she was quiet for a week. Lost in a dream world, contained to a single bedroom table.

Neighbors are not as understanding. In good times people are all Christian. Faith is easy, and judgment a hobby. She was no longer the troubled child—she was the trouble.

Her parents came to her. Initially it was: don't talk about the cards. Then: the cards stay in the house. Finally: *give us the cards.*

That was a fight to end all fights. She lost, of course. She learned to hate.

Hate is a precursor to love, in teenagers. The chemical capacity for love is there long before there's anyone to hold. Everything is Shakespeare for a few stormy years.

Deprived of tarot cards, Emily tried pot instead. It helped, actually; the visions were much gentler with pot. She wished she could cut them out of her head.

Until she got her wish.

15

"Salience," the doctor told them. "It's a matter of salience."

What a grand word. Father, mother, daughter waited for more.

"Our brain has to determine how salient something is, how much meaning to attach to it. For example, seeing an apple reminds you of William Tell. Do you dismiss that? Or do you suddenly worry you'll be shot with an arrow?"

Emily rolled her eyes. That was nothing like the frog.

"Or does William step out and start talking to you?"

Hmm.

"This is how schizophrenia works. Everything you see seems very real, because your brain treats every thought, every hunch as equal. It doesn't distinguish between the things that are actually there, and the things it wonders about."

Her dad shook his head. "Can you fix it?"

The doctor said he could.

He was mistaken.

16

The early treatments made it worse. She still saw everything, but now it was confused. She couldn't get the meaning. From Caterpillar she was reduced to wandering Alice.

It didn't really matter. She was already the outcast, the devil kid. They called her Wicked Witch at school. Or Crazy.

"Hey Crazy."

She was given her part and, dedicated artist that she was, she played it exactly as scripted. There is nothing to prove you are damaged goods like dressing as damaged goods.

Of course, what is designed to deter serves also as an advertisement, to a certain kind of man.

Joel wasn't a trouble kid. He was neither a bright student nor a washout. Athlete nor weakling. He got by, he took things easy. He seemed very safe.

Which he was, six days a week. Once in a while he snapped. That would drive off most people. Not Emily. She had the black shirt, the metal bits, the proactive sneer. She broadcast: "If you love me, you may hurt me." This was an acceptable offer.

He never hit her. He was not *so* easy to hate. But when he struck, he struck hard. And he struck often.

There were two ways Joel proved that he loved Emily. One

was tearful, passionate apologies. The other was fucking her with long, fast strokes.

He was a broken creature, like her. But he was *her* broken creature. He, at least, would never leave her.

And she wouldn't leave him, either.

17

She got pregnant one year after their first time. They were high school seniors. She denied it: first to herself, then to Joel, then to her parents. She looked up how to use herbs to abort a baby. But she didn't.

She had to stop her medication during the pregnancy. Things became very turbulent, very violent. Emily tried never to think of that year.

She was happy with her son, her beautiful son. He was the only thing she ever did right.

After becoming a mother she had one last fit of self-determination. She tried to start a business of her own. College was out, after all. And Joel stayed—of course he stayed—but how much did he earn? Not much.

Tarot cards scare good Christians, but not dowsers. She taught herself how in one day. She printed flyers and her dad put out the word. Old farmers respect dowsers.

There aren't many old farmers left.

Wells just aren't so hard anymore. You don't have to hand-dig anything. The well companies use maps, and they're not going to refer you to a lady with a rod. Wrong place? Oh well. The deeper they have to dig, the more they get to charge.

It took her another year to accept that she just wasn't going to make good as the Midwest's new water witch.

And so, unmarried, impecunious, imbalanced and unfulfilled, she began to raise a son. She lived with her parents, delighted in the boy, and slowly, slowly, learned to regard Joel not as her creature, but as a thorny and volatile necessity.

18

Emily's medication was finally sorted. Sometime around 20, they hit the right cocktail. Visions: gone. Voices: silenced. A universe of meta-data, courtesy not of computers but of authors unseen: 404.

This had its bleed. You cannot silence one feeling without silencing four others. Much of the world felt dead after that. Where she had once assigned too much salience, she now assigned too little. In short, she felt nothing.

It was not the worst thing she'd ever felt.

A few sharp feelings broke through: love of her son, distaste of Dad, fury for Joel. That about topped it.

But now there was a new feeling: worry.

She hadn't been worried in how long? Not that she was happy, comfortable, or safe—she was on the brink. But she was too stuffy in the head to feel fear. Until now.

The Devil card stared at her. The cards were only *symbols*, these days. Right? She read them mechanically, interpreted by textbook definition. She had seen the Devil before.

But this was *the Devil.*

She didn't want more devil.

She was late for work, and she put her cards away.

Part Three:
Strangers

19

The gentleman outside the café was, at best, strange.

If he had stepped out of a vehicle he would still be odd enough. A sober person does not look so haggard—but he hardly seemed drunk. He was more of an escaped hospital patient, a blood loss victim. Perhaps an addict.

But if this man was an unfit customer, the café was a perfect match. It was part of a downtown that once drew tourists, then served mostly locals, and now even the locals were absent. Someone had spent money to open it, but no one was spending to keep it alive. It was like a set in a depressing art film.

He leaned his bike against a tree where he could see it, and came inside.

20

Bailey fell into the café's booth. He released old man noises as he finally sat down.

The night had robbed him of his strength. Not enough of a storm to make him put up shelter. Just enough to leave him chilled. Chilled and aching against his tree.

A middle-aged woman came up and took his order. Her name tag read "Rachel."

"Coffee," he said.

"Aren't you going to order food?"

"Yes. But coffee, please."

She brought him coffee.

"What do you want to order, hon?"

He hadn't opened the menu. "Just give me some time, please. I'll order later."

"Hmm, okay."

All he really wanted was to sleep. But as soon as she went away he wondered if he'd been rude. He began to ponder this through heavy lids and heavy swallows of coffee.

Rachel stood at the counter and watched him. The other waitress showed up late. She was supposed to be there for lunch rush, which was a laugh.

"Who is that?" she asked.

"He came in on that bicycle," Rachel said.

The waitress looked scared.

Despite their precautions, the stranger perhaps sensed that they were talking about him. When Rachel came to refill his coffee for the third time, he apologized.

"I hope I wasn't rude before," he said.

"Oh, no!"

"I'm sorry."

"No, no. You must be real tired."

The man laughed. "Yeah."

He ordered a sandwich. For a while longer, he was left in peace.

When she came by to check on him he had mayo on his face.

"Is that your bike out there?"

He nodded, swallowing. "Yeah."

"Where you biking to?"

"Just biking, I guess."

"Just biking." She smiled. "Ha."

He was too tired to tell her his story. But also too tired to fend off her questions. How far do you go in a day? Where did you start? What do your parents think?

Then, finally:

"Where are you staying?"

"I don't know."

"Well where did you stay last night?"

He pondered how to answer. She named some town he never heard of. He shook his head.

"I slept under a tree."

Rachel laughed. Bailey did not. She hesitated.

"What, really?"

He nodded. "Yes."

She looked at him.

"What do you do? I mean, how do you, uh?"

"How do I support myself on the road?"

"Yeah."

He took a deep breath. Who knew how this would go.

"I cast spells."

They locked eyes, and there was silence.

Then:

"Do you really?"

He nodded. "I do. Really."

Rachel didn't know how to answer. She looked around. "Looks like you need some more water."

As soon as she was in the kitchen—which is not where water glasses are refilled—she seized the other waitress. They conferred.

The other waitress looked out the kitchen door. The stranger shoved french fries into his mouth. He was actually kind of cute.

21

Rachel and Bailey had a long conversation.

She had a TV view of magic. It was hard for him to relate to it, but it made her very excited.

He did his best to answer her questions.

Finally: "Where are you staying tonight?"

She had asked this before. That gave him hope. "Honestly? I don't know."

He was still tired, but he had perked up from the conversation. Rachel looked him up and down.

"Here's the thing," she said. "I have a good enough farm. I'm divorced now, but I have a lodger who keeps it going. There's room for another person there."

He didn't directly answer. Instead, he just waited.

"If you want to stay there you can."

Once, Bailey would have been far too polite. He would try to refuse, make her offer again.

"I'd love that," he said.

22

Rachel had to finish her shift first. She felt awkward that Bailey would have to wait, but he had nothing else to do. He found a book to read and settled in.

Lunch did actually bring some customers. Enough to ward off bankruptcy? No, but a few.

As the lunch rush faded, Rachel vanished to do her side work. The other waitress was still there.

All morning she had shot him sideways looks. The kind of looks you shoot when you think your target is unaware. He *was* aware, eventually. He caught her and smiled. She ran away into the kitchen.

When she had to pass by his table, he flagged her down.

"What's this town like?" he asked.

She cringed.

"It's a piece of shit."

He laughed. She laughed too.

"It's true!"

"What, exactly, makes this fine town a piece of shit?"

He motioned out the window. It offered a view of a Dairy Queen, two bars, a check cashing business, four closed businesses, and a library only open 12 hours a week.

She kept on laughing.

"You would have to grow up here," she said.

"You just can't appreciate it. I slept under a *tree* last night."

"That actually sounds kind of nice."

"You know, it actually is." He said it as a joke but then smiled a real smile.

"What's all this crap about doing magic?" she asked.

He shrugged and smiled. "It's what I do."

"So you can make anything happen, huh?"

"Well... anything *could* happen. Whether *I* make it or not..." he shook his head.

"Sounds like a bullshitter."

He leaned in. "You know what?" he whispered. "It *does* sound like that."

He grinned and her. She grinned back.

They both laughed.

Someone at another table was trying very, very hard to get the waitress's attention. She finally accepted.

"I have to go. You're staying at Rachel's place?"

"That's the plan," he agreed. "I'm Bailey."

He stuck out his hand. She took it.

"I'm Emily."

Part Four:
Seeds

23

It was a bad week for advertising.

The ad man only needed one farm. One farm doing well. He had gone to each customer, first the big ones then the little ones. They had all purchased the Granta Patented Designer Drought Resistant Seeds, and he expected to find some fairly lush fields. Instead he found anger.

One woman called him "the whore of Satan's dog." As if he had designed them! He was just trying to sell them. Another family literally chased him with dogs. He had a stack of complaint forms riding in the passenger seat. It was a bad week.

He pulled his truck up alongside a tract of soybean field. The poor little plants looked like someone had gone after them with a hair dryer. Like the ground had been salted. No, then it would be a pretty white. The soil—where he could see it, which was most places—was blonde with sand. It never fully recovered from last year's floods, and then this drought came.

It was the same everywhere.

These soybean plants were doomed. He didn't even talk to the customer. Instead he marked a survey map with "sand—fucked." They didn't really need a soy farmer anyway. They needed a corn farmer.

He laughed, alone in his truck.

Granta didn't have a winning product, so it needed a poster child. Someone who *looked* like a winner.

Out here, there were only losers.

24

Rachel's farm was outside town. They followed a wooded road up a slight hill. In three miles they found a gravel road. They were home.

The house was on one side of the gravel road, set way back with trees for privacy. Her fields were on the other side.

Near the house was a shed, which was also a garage and a laundry room, depending on which door you entered. Behind that were chicken houses and enclosed pools for ducks. An ancient barn loomed nearby.

The house was rustic outside but carefully kept inside. Rachel treated knickknacks like relics.

The fields across the road were pasture. On this side was corn. Bailey felt very peaceful as they pulled up. Only minutes later did he realize how *green* the corn was.

He unloaded the bicycle from Rachel's truck. She told him to put it in the garage. When he came back out, she was talking to another man his age.

Jacob took care of the farm. Rachel had no interest in farming; that was a dream that died with her marriage. It was a small operation, and Jacob handled it all himself or arranged for help when needed. In exchange he got food and a bedroom.

"Bailey's going to be staying here for a few days," Rachel said. Bailey had thought it was just for the night. He didn't argue.

Jacob nodded. "Sure. Well, make yourself at home. There's some fresh milk in the fridge, but it's not pasteurized if that matters to you."

Rachel told Jacob about the café being dead again. Jacob had no pity for the owner; he had some angry words about the place's business practices.

"You're making Bailey uncomfortable!"

At the same time, both Bailey and Jacob shrugged.

"Well, you probably want to get cleaned up," Rachel said, "And rest. We'll have dinner in a bit."

"I'd like that. But I'm happy to help out with chores. I don't mind working."

Jacob repeated his shrug. "There's not much to do. I'm going to go out with the cows in a bit. You can come along if you like."

Bailey showered, and he did just that.

25

"You don't have fences?"

Bailey was no farmer, but he knew you need fences.

"You don't really need them," Jacob said. "We only have three cows, and they mostly stay on our pasture. I kind of keep an eye on them."

Bailey looked across the gravel road at the green corn stalks, and across the highway at a much larger field of brown corn.

"Don't they get into the corn?"

"Once in a while. Just ours. They don't like crossing the highway."

He gestured out at the pasture. It was a dense few acres of native tangle.

"I raise cows the way they would live in the wild. They have everything they want here. We don't try to cheat them."

The cattle were in the middle of the tangle, near the highway side. They seemed to have no interest in crossing the roads. It was a mom and two calves.

"So this is all organic?"

Jacob made a face. He took on his heated voice. "Organic is bullshit. It's a term they use in marketing. The requirements for organic come nowhere near what's actually natural."

He seemed to forcibly cool his voice. "I mean, organic is better than most of the stuff they sell at the store. I understand why people want it. It's just you can do a lot of really wicked stuff to an animal or the land and still get your organic certification."

Bailey nodded, thinking about it.

The cows were used to Jacob and they started to move with him a little bit as he approached. The two men began to guide the cattle on a long, very slow circuit of the pasture.

"It looks like your corn is pretty green, too."

"Yeah. It's not great, with the drought, but it's hanging in there. We'll probably be down ten percent or so from what we'd expect."

"Compared to everything else I've seen..."

Jacob pointed across the highway. "You see that?"

"Yeah."

"Genetically modified. Super seed, made in a lab. Every kernel's the same."

"So when something goes wrong—"

"It kills all of them. Yeah." Then he pointed at his own field. "Our seeds are as mixed up as wildflowers. It's a little bit of everything. A drought can't kill them all."

Bailey nodded. "You did it all natural."

"All native. These plants have survived a prairie summer before. Tens of thousands of years."

"Hmm."

Bailey began to understand why he felt so at home.

26

Dinner was ready. Jacob took his and went outside. Bailey was done with outside for a little.

"Do you want a beer?" Rachel asked.

"That would be amazing. Thank you."

"Jacob doesn't like it when I drink. He says it's not healthy."

"Well."

"He's all about the healthy. And he only wants to eat what we grow here. But I like beer and chocolate."

"You could probably brew your own beer."

She waved her hand like the whole idea exhausted her.

The meal she made was good. "Do you like it?" she asked. Her eyes glowed when he said yes.

"So tell me about these spells. Do you think you could do something for the farm?"

"Probably. What do you need?"

"Well, our corn is really struggling with the drought. Everyone's is."

Bailey almost answered wrong: *Jacob said yours is doing fine.* He hadn't; he said it would be down ten percent.

"I'll go out tonight and do a blessing for it."

"Will that help?"

Bailey leaned back. "I— well, there are a lot of traditional charms for crops. It was one of the biggest uses of magic, once."

She looked at him like she had caught him.

"You don't sound so sure."

"I'll have to see what we're dealing with."

27

Actually Bailey wasn't so sure.

He had never done a charm for crops before. More important, he wasn't sure it was possible.

The thing is: how does magic *work*? Bailey knew a dozen theories. They all sounded a little made up.

One theory says it works by the power of belief. So a love spell makes you go out and try harder to meet someone. A money spell makes you work harder or look for more opportunities. It's in your head.

But dying crops are not in your head.

He wasn't sure he could do it. Aximander appeared beside him; *Why not?* the wolf seemed to say.

Bailey crossed the yard, picking up a stick as he went. Two farm dogs regarded him as he passed, giving some half-hearted yaps. He was old news.

I don't know what I'm doing, he thought.

Of course you do.

What if I can't do it? What if my magic doesn't work?

Aximander disappeared.

It wasn't the first time he'd wondered. But in college he didn't *need* the magic. If it was all in his head, all just a hobby, it was no big deal.

Now people wanted to count on him. What if Rachel had a bad harvest? How much of her income was that? Bailey didn't know.

I thought you were a wizard.

Bailey sighed.

He thought so too.

28

A stranger in town. Staying at Rachel's. It didn't take long for the news to spread.

And of course, that wasn't all.

They were drinking. Rather, Rachel and Bailey were drinking. Jacob excused himself. He knew his path in life: back to nature. He talked about hunter gatherers, about raw food, about what cooking food does to your body. Everything he said came with the raised, set jaw of certainty. And the proof of his convictions was in his body. Shirtless, he was like a statue; clothed, like a model.

Rachel couldn't be more different. She was thin but soft, happy but easily alarmed. She'd raised a son who was off doing what escapees do. She shared a dream with a man, once, and now the man was gone. She had no sail to catch the wind. No pennant, perhaps, to show the way.

In every way she was the less certain, less determined, perhaps less impressive of the two. But she also had affection and curiosity. She had warmth. These were things Jacob lacked, because he knew only one road. Jacob had Fate; Rachel had friends.

Bailey didn't mind when Jacob excused himself.

But the conversation with Rachel was interrupted by a phone call two beers in. Rachel found her way to the kitchen to answer it, Bailey sat back heavily in the chair and felt his knotted muscles shake.

Words from the kitchen caught him.

"Oh yes, he is staying here!"

A pause.

"Haha, yes, that's what he says. I was just talking with him —"

"Well I don't know. He says they do."

"I bet he would do that! Yes of course!"

Bailey did not like that. He almost got up.

"Well you're welcome to come over now if you want but let the man rest. He biked all the way here. Haha no I guess not!"

"Alright. I'll tell him. I can give him a ride over tomorrow. Sure, love you sweetheart. See you then."

The phone clacked back into its place on the wall. An old fashioned phone. Rachel came skipping back, new beer in hand.

"Hey, Mister Magician! You just got a customer!"

Mister Magician asked for another beer.

29

Bailey asked the man what was in his garage. He found a piece of canvas, an old tarpaulin, and unfurled it. He also found wood, house paint and clear varnish.

He had not accepted the ride. In the morning he asked for directions and took his bike. It was nine miles.

"Does it really work?" the man asked.

"I don't know," Bailey said.

"How much do you charge?"

"Pay me what you think is right."

The man nodded.

Bailey folded over the edge of the canvas like a hem. He used the varnish like glue. Then he took a nail and began piercing holes along the hem. The man had watched intently to this point; now he intervened.

"Do you want an awl?"

"If you have one."

An awl appeared.

With the holes punched he grabbed bailing twine to lash the canvass to a piece of wood. He looked at it. Scroll, or flag?

A glance up at the man. His wife was dying. He needed a source of hope. Flag, obviously.

Bailey used a longer piece of wood and attached the canvas as a flag. Then he mixed paint with a variety of ingredients. He sent the man into the house for kitchen herbs. He asked for soil of different kinds.

"Do you have booze?"

Nod.

"Bring that out."

The man not only brought the bottle, he made two margaritas for them, too.

Bailey lit a fire in the fire pit and combined things. He burnt offerings, he scraped soot. The soot went into a paste. The paste acted like a pigment, dark outlines around the painted areas. Slowly the marching banner of a long forgotten deity took its shape, with flourishes.

Many times the man offered him sweets. For a meal, out came commercially prepared pastries. Bailey gave them to Aximander.

He set his jaw like Jacob's. A honed professional at work. His face, complete confidence. Inside: did he really think this would save a life?

He couldn't lie. He had quit that career. He called the man over.

"Three things," he said.

The man waited.

"Keep going to the doctor and do whatever they say."

The man kept waiting.

"That's important, get it?"

"Sure. Of course."

"Okay. Stop eating so many sweets."

"What?"

"Seriously."

76

Slow nodding.

"Okay, and make regular offerings at this flag. The spirits like offerings. Maybe pour out a little tequila or something. Put some food out."

The man had a dozen questions about that, which Bailey answered.

The flag was placed over the door of the house. The clear varnish wasn't even dry when the wind caught it. It looked like folk art from another country. At the same time, in the afternoon light, it looked regal. Glowed. The colors were bold; the only kind Bailey knew to use. It was magical, or at least haunted.

The man was nervous.

"I, uh, I want to invite you in for dinner, but I can't explain to her what we did."

"That's fine. I think I'm going to bike home."

Home.

"You want a ride? I'll give you a ride."

"No, biking sounds great."

Bailey leaned in.

"Look. I don't know what's going to happen with her. I don't like to make promises I can't keep. But I can tell you someone else is working for her. Keep offering to that spirit, and he'll keep his hand on her shoulder."

He made long eye contact with the man. Bailey's eyes said: *I'm trying my best. Thank you.* The man's eyes said: *No one tries for us. Thank you.*

Evening set in on the road. The cool breeze felt good. It soothed his body but not his conscience. Why did that man believe him? Did he believe himself?

The eyes had been relieved, grateful. He remembered the eyes, and maybe it was okay.

30

Life went on like that. One day he painted a giant sigil on the side of a barn (in whitewash!). Another day he made a string of beads with a little charm at the end. He always used what his customers had to hand, and he always required their help in some way. It was excellent work.

Aximander became more and more real in his mind. He began to feel the spirit, tangibly, when he fell asleep and when he awoke. At times the pup stayed close; other times he went away. Rather than bigger, he grew more substantial.

Bailey enchanted for many problems, and people found reasons to believe it worked, as they do. But his most popular request was the one he kept refusing.

"Can you save the corn crop?"

"Maybe. I'm working on it."

Working on it meant walking in the fields alone. The trick was feeling what Rachel's land had—really what *Jacob's* land had —that the others didn't.

It wasn't something he could transfer over.

He had two options. He could tell them he was no miracle worker, sorry; or give them the same half-promise he had given the man with the sick wife.

Or find a way to fix it.
But there wasn't one.

31

Days passed. A week. Rachel was happy for the company; the town was happy for the novelty.

Bailey's customers were spread over half a county. The roads were built for cars: too few total and only connected in far-flung ways. And some connections were just gravel, which Bailey's road bike did not like. As a result, the magician frequently coasted into town on one main road to pick up another out into the country.

This brought him near the café.

It became his habit to stop there and rest. He would be sweaty from the sun, and they had air conditioning that wasn't *too* cold. A little money coming in, no rent to pay. And he liked talking to the waitress.

One day he was the only customer. Emily brought him an iced tea.

"You don't look happy," she said.

He nodded. He had listened to over an hour of talk about corn at the last farm. It was all explained in much detail, in an effort to convince him to do something. The summer heat was not so wilting as the *need*.

"It's been a rough day."

Emily looked at the café door. No one was coming.

"Guess what," she said.

He looked up. "What?"

Her hand slid underneath her waitress apron and produced a small metal flask.

She smiled. So did he.

Bailey accepted the flask and unstopped it, neither asking nor sniffing. He just upended it and took a hit.

The face he made set Emily laughing. "You could've asked for some coke."

He breathed out fumes. "Is that 151?"

"Fuck *yes*." She stole back the opened flask and took a hit of her own. She leaned against the wall of the booth. "How do people not hate you?"

He tilted his head. She laughed.

"I mean! No. I mean this is a really Christian town."

"You're right. I should introduce myself to the pastor."

"Ugh, don't bother." She sipped her rum again. "No one told you you're going to Hell?"

"Not to my face." He shrugged. "I'm sure they say it."

Emily said some things about religion. Bailey just listened.

"I think they're accepting because it's bad times," he said at last. "What they've got isn't working."

"No one knows you. They have to be nice to you because you're a guest."

"Yeah, I am. So give me some more rum."

She leaned over in a very intentional way. He took a slow swig.

"Everybody has problems," he said at last. "I try to help them fix it. If I was just some guy doing spooky things, I'd be cold shouldered out of town. But I offer to help, and they like

82

that."

Emily frowned.

32

There were clouds, but no rain. Days came and days went.

Portions of cropland looked like beach.

The corn didn't put out tassels. Without tassels, there was no pollination. Without pollination the ears can't form.

Some turned to their crop insurance. The insurance companies wouldn't pay, or not yet. They needed to see final results. But the farmers had been through this before: claims would be denied, delayed, underpriced.

Some mulched their fields. Preparation for next year. Others didn't bother.

There were clouds but no rain.

Part Five:
Wind

33

Emily couldn't see it from her window.

Her dad had made a smart decision. Like most farms, they were limited in irrigation. You just can't cover all your acres every day all summer long. The equipment has to be moved from section to section to share the water around.

Or you can triage.

Park the irrigators on one field and save it, let the others dry up. Four times out of five it's a bad tactic. A little rain will come here and there, and if you keep moving those irrigators you can save the whole crop.

But he had been doing this his whole life, and he sensed the one time in five. He chose the front field that was easily accessible and irrigated it. Everything else he cut loose.

Now their land looked like tinder on three sides. Only the front of the farm had any green. Emily's room faced away.

She was okay with that. Tensions were already high, but Dad could look out his window and see the green and that gave him less worry. But it also meant she couldn't see Joel's car coming. Whenever she heard the dogs barking her heart leapt up in her chest. She held her breath.

She didn't want another fight.

34

"I'm going to talk to that stranger."

Emily's heart stuttered.

"Wh, why?"

Her father had been sitting at the kitchen table for hours. He'd made a bunch of phone calls that morning in his work room with the door closed. Since then he sat there with bills and financial records in complete silence.

He looked angry at the question.

"He's supposed to be some kind of miracle worker."

"I don't think that's for real," she said.

Dad looked suspicious. Emily believed in this stuff.

She went on. "I see him all the time at the café. He's just some guy from the city."

Dad chewed on that.

She decided to push her point. "I could do a better job myself."

That was a poor choice.

"Oh, you're a gypsy again?"

"Dad—"

He shook his head angrily. "If you had some kinda spell you should've used it already. But you don't. Doctor said it's all in your head."

He eyes burned. She could only raise her voice.

"Well *he* doesn't either!"

Dad never raised his voice. He just got up and walked out.

35

That week the requests became too much. Bailey had to give the farmers something: he couldn't promise a fix, but he at least had to act.

"I'll come out and take a look." So he did.

He walked the land. He cleared his mind like he would to make offerings. He let himself feel beyond what he felt. Open to the land.

It was dust, it was bitter, it was poison.

Like putting an acorn in your mouth. There is something nutritious there, something worth eating. But the flavor is too bitter, too dry. You can't swallow. It parches you. You spit it on the ground and look for water.

There's a way to prepare acorns. You can leach out the bitter till there's only goodness left. But the goodness of the land was all used up. If there was a way to restore it, it was not in a day, not in a week, not in a spell. It was jacked up on false seeds and strange chemicals. Nothing numinous left to save.

"I'm sorry," he told the farmer. It was the first time he gave a straight answer. "This is beyond what I can do. It's too late."

The farmer didn't want to believe it. He pushed for options, alternatives, "try anyway." It was always *try anyway*. Listen, I told you. It's not going to work.

So he wanted reasons.

"It's.... your land. It doesn't feel natural anymore. The life isn't in the land. I don't know if it's just the drought or if it's... well."

"If it's what?"

"If it's the chemicals and seeds you're using."

There was a lot of glaring. Bailey thought he crossed a line. He didn't know anything about agriculture. He just knew the land here was not happy. He said as much.

That man was not angry at his wizard. He was angry at the seed company and the chemical company. All farmers knew it was bad, but they had to use it anyway. They had to stay competitive.

Bailey left quickly and quietly. He managed another "I'm sorry." But that wasn't what stuck with the farmer.

What he told the other men at the tavern was, "He said the land is dead."

"That's your land. What about my land?"

"Didn't say."

36

Two nights later Bailey came into the café. The sun had just set. The town was lit with that pink-gray gloam that closes a summer dusk. The air was cool, breathy, full of grit. There were still three kids in the park. Probably they were drinking. Everything else was quiet, which is not how late summer nights should be.

Emily was about to close. If it was dead she could close up early. She had put it off, because she didn't want to go home. But when she saw Bailey she wished she had left.

"We're closed," she said.

He sat down at the counter. "Okay."

"We're closed, you have to go."

He looked at her with heavy, weary eyes. She really didn't want his eyes to leave.

"I'm gonna sit here while you do your work," he said. "I'm gonna take a rest."

Dammit. That was reasonable.

"Do you want anything?"

"I thought you were closing."

"I'm trying to be fucking nice."

"Milkshake."

"No."

"Root beer."

"Fine."

She came back and put a Coors on the counter. His eyes closed halfway and his face turned into a soft smile.

"Thanks."

"Why are you so beat?"

"Everybody wants me to save the corn. Or the soybeans."

"So do it."

He drank a long, hard pull of the beer. Swallowed purposefully. "I can't."

Laughter. She *fucking* laughed.

She was bent down putting something under the counter, or getting something out, and she didn't even look at him. She just laughed.

"Bullshit," she said.

He looked down at her, almost angry.

"If you believe you can do it, you can do it," she said. "That's how magic works."

"*That's* bullshit."

He swallowed another quarter of the beer. Then he kept talking.

"It's not some positive thinking crap. You need to put something *in* to get something out." He spoke louder as she walked into the kitchen, carrying a tray of coffee mugs. "And the land here is just *fucked*. It's just fucked, Em. Everyone wants me to fix it and I can't."

She stared at him from the kitchen doorway.

"Did you just call me *Em?*"

He grinned.

Bailey finished his beer. He stood up. "Let me help you with the chores."

"Side work."

"Right."

"Well come and get it."

He was tired and buzzed but it felt good to stand up. He came around the counter. The plan was to take the other mugs. Instead he grabbed her shoulder.

There was no doubt in him.

She pulled away. "Don't!"

Bailey stepped back. Her hair was disheveled. Her face was flushed. The point of a nipple showed through her shirt.

He tilted his head at her like a cat.

"Don't."

A car horn honked. Emily looked anxiously at the café door. Bailey did not.

"That's my boyfriend," she said firmly.

He laughed. "You have a boyfriend?"

She just glared at him.

37

Her son was asleep. He didn't usually take afternoon naps, but today she managed to get him down. It was good, because she needed the time alone.

She held a string of beads. They were carved and lacquered before she was born, lacquered bright red. The red had faded, tarnished, darkened. They belonged to her grandmother. Gran was no longer part of this world, but she too had worried for a child, worried for a man, worried for her own future.

Emily talked to her now.

"If you're there, Gran..."

Gran was not there. It was an empty, silent room. But Emily carried her, carried her in the loneliness.

"If you're there, I want you to know I'm scared. And I know you ran off to the city when you were scared. And you met Grandpa and everything worked out for you. But I don't think it's going to work out for me.

"I would leave tomorrow, if it was just me. I don't care what happens to me. I would leave Joel and go. But I have a kid. I have to stay. I have to stay, right?"

She breathed in. She held that breath, as if waiting for Gran to answer back. Gran did not answer. Yet Emily felt she was not alone.

She froze. Only her eyes moved to the side, swung to look at the intruder. It was something half-there. Her heart stopped in fear, but it wasn't there to harm her. A hallucination? She hadn't had a hallucination in years. And this, whatever it was, did not give her paranoia. Instead, reassurance.

Then the spirit moved. A sudden step that took it right out her door. She was on her feet immediately. Should she follow? Of course—she *needed* to.

Emily didn't see it in the hall. But her old ways came back to her, and she felt with a sense she thought was burned shut. She knew she had to go down the hall, down the stairs, out the back; she was happy no one was there.

Outside she was less certain. She saw movement in the dry, dead corn. It could have just been a bird, but she decided to believe it was the spirit.

Emily almost fell. She had to put one hand on the porch post. She swooned; a presence coursed through her; she sobbed without sadness.

Oh God I missed you.

She used to feel spirits all the time and she missed them so, so much.

When she gathered herself, she took off into the corn at a fast run. She didn't know where she was going, but she *would* know.

The corn was too short. It should have been over her head. Wisps of not-silk crumbled and fried off as she pushed through. The air was full of it, hazy and gold and hot and dry. The fields literally crackled around her.

The place she stopped was the old cotton willow. It crowned a small hill between two fields. Tall grass and weeds surrounded it; they did better than the corn. The grass was brown and sharp. At the foot of the tree there was nothing growing at all.

There was the spirit.

Standing, proud, unafraid. Visible. She stared. It stared back.

Emily dropped to the soil. Hot tears fell down her face. The first water in three months. The soil could barely even hold it.

She sobbed and then wept, deep tears for herself, her boy, her lost dreams and visions.

She spoke to it out loud:

"I don't... want. You to go."

The tears kept falling. She knew it would go. She knew before she even said the words. But she didn't want her visions to stop once again.

She held out the beads with both hands. She dropped them in the bare soil, dropped them in two coils. A gift, an offering, anything.

The spirit paused in leaving. It looked back at her. It looked like a dog. A white dog. Or something like that.

38

Bailey rose before dawn. This was not pleasant for him; a cheerful Jacob made it no easier.

He ate no breakfast and mounted his bike. It was six miles to the church. There were several churches in the area, but only one was a quaint old country church from a hundred years ago. To Bailey that was "the church."

Six miles is a nice little ride on a summer morning. It woke him up. Dew hung in the air, taunting the farmers, refreshing the magus. The sun rose behind a few clouds. The clouds moved on.

He went nowhere near the church. Instead he leaned his bike against a churchyard gate. There he laid down offerings: four splashes of water, a handful of oats, and some whiskey. He knelt at the gate and said his welcomes to the dead.

Bailey had never been here. He knew the place. He stooped down and removed his shoes and socks. Barefoot, the grass felt wet and cold. It bit into his skin.

He had nowhere to put his shoes so he slung them over his shoulder, dangling them from two fingers.

The path was gravel. He winced, he kept walking. The churchyard was lovely. Old markers, flowers he couldn't name.

He made his way past the trees till he could see the sunrise. One side was a row of oaks; the other, the church.

He knelt and began. Words rose to heavens, his chant to his god. He declared it loudly, boldly; he did not care who overheard. Anyway they were asleep.

"Apollo—!"

The words grew higher; he called down that ancient name, renewed his pledge. When the words ended he prostrated before the sun. Two hands pressed in grass and flowers. He shivered with the cold of the earth and the burn of the light. He stretched there, alive.

A murmur:

"Bathe my face in fire,
Cense me in perfume,
In the ancient way,
Oh! In the ancient way,
In the ancient way
I place signs upon my hands,
Signs upon my hands,
Your magician, Apollo,
There are signs upon my hands..."

He chanted and he drew.

With his right finger he drew on his left palm. It was covered in soil, loose dusty soil. The sigil took form stroke by stroke. It bristled in the hand.

Then he drew on the other hand. The symbols were not the same.

Breathless he invoked their spells. Two powers to surround him all day and all night. Till again, in the morning, he faced the sun and prayed. And he would: he would pray every day. Every day, he would enchant.

The hands clapped together. A crow landed above. It chanted, too, and he smiled.

"Is there any farm, Apollo, that I can save?"

Emily's words haunted him. *If you believe it, you can do it. That's how magic works.*

Apollo did not disagree. The crow had nothing more to say. Aximander stood by, at some nearby grave.

"*Is* there?"

He tried to clear his mind. Nothing. He looked again at the crow, again at the sun, and Aximander heeled beside him.

He blinked in the bright light. In one blink, one image. A blood-red cross: a blood-red X.

Bailey paused. His mouth opened, but no question came forth. His forehead wrinkled in thought. At last he nodded, and prostrated one last time.

Charmed, he stood.

Leaving the church-yard he saw the pastor. The man watched him without critique. But what a sight: dirt on the hands, face, lips, knees. Barefoot, red scratches. Shoes slung over one side.

"Good morning," Bailey said.

"Good morning," the pastor said. "Will you be joining us for service today?"

"No, but thank you very much. I said my morning prayers."

39

That day another farmer approached Bailey, with the same request as always.

This time, Bailey said he would be happy to help. The man looked suspicious.

Bailey took his address, and said he would come after supper.

40

"Will this work?" the farmer asked Bailey.

"I don't know," he said. He was sincerely intrigued to try.

"What will it cost?"

"Nothing. I don't even know if it will work."

"If it works, I gotta pay you."

"I accept."

That was all their conversation; the man asked what Bailey needed and he said he needed to walk their land. The farmer nodded and went back to the stack of bills on the kitchen table.

The crops out front were in good shape. They were well watered. The irrigators hung over them like bridges, like stalkers. It was one green, gold field lining the front road. Bailey went there first.

The irrigators had a way of moving, slowly. You could mistake them for dinosaurs. Somehow the water pressure or a timer or a motor turned their wheels here and there, and they inched over the crops with their life-saving cloud.

Bailey got sprayed a little. It was nice. His shirt wet against his skin. The water dripped from poor fittings on the irrigators; it wasn't wasted.

The land here felt good. Not perfect, still forced into its way by unnatural agriculture. But it had something to give. Concentrating: which way did the life run?

It was there, it was deep down. He began to follow it. He never could have found it if he didn't know what to look for. Whether it could be saved, that was different. He had doubts but he had to find the blood-red X.

Aximander trotted. Not leading, but certainly knowing the way.

As he walked Bailey chanted. He began an old lay used to bless the land in spring in Scotland. When he finished that chant, he began the song to summon rain. The wind picked up. There were clouds today: a man could hope.

Bailey was very much not looking around him. He did not know that the waitress, Emily, was in the same field. He just sang over and over.

Aximander vanished, there was a scraping in the corn, a fluttering of birds taking flight. This attracted Bailey's gaze, and Emily's.

One saw the other.

The two had different reactions. Bailey continued singing but stared, perplexed, taking far too long to realize she must live on this farm.

Emily's eyes flashed anger. She waffled whether to run or to go chase him off; she started toward him.

"What are you *doing* here?" she demanded in a scream.

Bailey did not stop his song. He looked at her, as if he was singing to *her*, not to the nine elements.

"What are you doing? Why are you here?"

He finished the last line, took a swig of whiskey, and spat it on the ground. Then he bowed formally to her.

"I'm setting a spell on your farm."

"We don't *need* any spells."

"I was told otherwise."

"I can do the spells around here! We don't need any spells!"

A smile betrayed him. "Those are two different answers. They don't even go together."

"YOU HAVE TO LEAVE."

He didn't feel that was true. He wondered briefly if he should have put a spell on *her*. Without backing down, he opened his mouth to answer. She snarled.

Pitter.

Bailey froze. Then put a hand to his face.

"What are you doing?" she asked.

"I think... I think I felt a rain drop."

"Bullshit. Go. *Now!*"

Patter.

Bailey looked up at the sky. The clouds were thin and pale. But maybe?

Thap.

It was audible. A rain drop on dry, rusty soil.

Emily stepped closer as if to say something. Her eyes were on him, intense, uncertain.

The rain started to come down. Emily put out her hand to see it, and Bailey grabbed it. Before she could move, they were kissing.

It was long and slow and firm. When they broke away, they held each other and watched it fall. Emily didn't believe it. She was warm in his arms.

"Let's get out of the rain," Bailey said. A silly thing to say. Neither of them minded the wet. He started toward a tree.

41

At the foot of the cotton willow was a string of red beads. They stopped Bailey's beating heart. Emily said some nervous words; he didn't hear them. Bailey looked at her and made up his mind. He wrapped his hand through her hair.

The other hand touched her hip. Then he knew the rest of the spell.

First they kissed standing up. Then he pressed her against the tree trunk. Finally he helped her to the ground, her hips beside the beads. Her dress was almost invisible from the rain. He pulled off the panties and they took each other on the bare earth, in the way of the pagans.

They made hungry love. Emily had not slept with her man in months. Bailey had not had a woman since before biking. She threw her hips up against him, she fucked back, hard. He pinned her to the land, and they made grooves in the earth.

"I'm not— on anything," she breathed.

He bit her neck.

She began to grind on every stroke. The sun cut through the falling rain. Hot mist rose on the fields.

Emily did not know what she was doing. Her emotions hadn't caught up to her. In the end, she took the devil card and played it.

Nails scratched into Bailey's back. Legs locked around him, she dragged her face to his ear.

"Inside me," she whispered.

His eyes were closed. "No."

He took his time. He pressed her back against the earth, he pushed her fingers down onto herself. As her body shook he pushed her thighs apart, and leaned away.

He leaned away, and between her legs he sprayed jets of semen onto the ground. Much of it was on her, but much was on the land.

42

Emily gasped. She looked at him with love.

"Did you—? You're—?"

He pulled her by the shoulder to sit up. "Enchant with me," he managed.

She sat with legs lewdly splayed. His tool dropped and the head touched the soil. He took her hand and they drew a circle in earth.

Bailey reached for a string of blood red beads under brown grass.

"What are you doing?" she asked.

"We need these." He held up the string. It had stopped raining.

Bailey went to tear the string of beads, to liberate them.

"Those were my grandma's!"

He stopped. He gave her a strange look, then nodded.

"Alright," he said.

He folded them into two loops, so they crossed in the middle and made a red X. This he placed on the seed in the center of the circle.

"Say the words with me."

She nodded. He said a line; she said a line. The words came

easily to both of them, and they kissed.

"This will save the farm?"

"Yes. I think it will."

43

It was time to go. Bailey lashed his gear onto his bicycle. The short rain storm had not helped one bit. Emily's crop, and all the corn crops, were failed.

But the ad man made out. He got a bonus in a bad year. Granta's product had failed every one of their customers, but it was a PR victory.

He'd found a farm with a huge successful corn field out front. They weren't even Granta customers, they just irrigated the hell out of it. The ad man approached the farm owner about putting Granta signs all along his stretch of ripe, roadfront corn. They even did a photo shoot to use for publicity.

The farmer bargained up the price, and Granta paid it.

Emily put her son into the car. He asked her again where they were going. She put a finger to his lips and closed the door.

Her dad had tried to pay Bailey, but he'd refused.

"I can always enchant up some money if I have to," he had said, and he believed that. "Give it to someone who needs it."

When Bailey left it was a beautiful September day. The evenings had a chill now, and he got an early start. Pedaling warmed him up.

He stopped near Emily's farm. He stood with one foot on the ground, the other on a pedal, and he looked out over the land.

The back fields had all been mulched. The cotton willow stood alone, reigning over hungry mice and birds. Its cotton drifted on the wind, carried over his head, off to fall wherever it may.

He breathed in deeply the last air of summer. Then movement drew his eye.

Down the road behind him, a car pulled out of Emily's long winding drive. It stopped while the driver checked for traffic. She looked up the road and she saw a stranger on a bike.

Neither Emily nor Bailey could see each other's face. But they each saw the other's eyes.

The car pulled out onto the road, turned away. The sound of the engine grew softer and softer.

Bailey let it go, and kicked into motion.

He followed the cotton willow, and followed the wind.

He followed the wind of fate.

This book is dedicated to everyone who helped me in 1,800 miles of biking.

ABOUT DREW JACOB

Drew Jacob is a wandering philosopher who believes adventure can change and improve lives. Although he was trained as a priest, founded a polytheist temple, and built a career in non-profits, he gave it all up to put his ideas to the test.

Drew's work has earned him a place as a contributing scholar at State of Formation, a project of the Journal of Inter-Religious Dialogue, and as a columnist at Patheos.org. He was chosen to speak at the first Hero Round Table, a cross-disciplinary conference on creating real heroism in today's world. He has never done anything heroic, but follows the path the ancient heroes took.

Slowly Drew is making his way 8,000 miles to Brazil by bicycle and by foot. Originally from Brew City, he now has no permanent home and no plans to get one. He writes dispatches from his Journey every week at RoguePriest.net.

www.ingramcontent.com/pod-product-compliance
Lightning Source LLC
Chambersburg PA
CBHW070341130626
46556CB00007B/2971

* 9 780099 200 5 948 *